Printed in the United States of America   •   First Edition   •   1 3 5 7 9 10 8 6 4 2   •   F322-8368-0-13135

Library of Congress Cataloging-in-Publication Data
Pace, Anne Marie.
Vampirina ballerina hosts a sleepover / written by Anne Marie Pace ; pictures by LeUyen Pham.—First edition.   p.   cm.
Summary: "Before Vampirina can host her very first sleepover there are a few things she must keep in mind: be polite and offer her guests food (like blood pudding); plan some games like scavenger hunt (but keep the clues simple so no one gets lost); and don't forget to dance! Vampirina may be a little nervous at first, but by following a few simple rules she will host the Best Sleepover Ever!"—Provided by publisher.
ISBN 978-1-4231-7570-4 (hardback)
[1. Sleepovers—Fiction. 2. Vampires—Fiction.] I. Pham, LeUyen, illustrator. II. Title.
PZ7.P113Vbh 2013   [E]—dc23   2013000652

Designed by Michelle Gengaro-Kokmen   •   Text is set in 22-point Rolando Opti   •   Art is created using watercolor and pen-and-ink on Strathmore paper
Reinforced binding   •   Visit www.disneyhyperionbooks.com

VAMPIRINA BALLERINA
HOSTS A SLEEPOVER

WRITTEN BY Anne Marie Pace

PICTURES BY LeUyen Pham

Disney•HYPERION BOOKS
New York

If you want to host the best sleepover ever for the best friends ever, you have to plan ahead.

Start with invitations, so everyone
knows what, when, and where.

While some hosts buy them,

I suggest
making your own;

it's far more festive,

and everyone will think they're a scream.

If you invite a new friend,

don't be surprised if her parents want
to meet yours before the party.

Take advantage of the visit.
Use the time to concoct your sleepover strategy.

Of course, bringing those ideas to life
means a long to-do list.

You'll need to cook up a menu,

shop for
supplies,

and spruce up your surroundings

with fabulous party decor.

That way, on the night
of the sleepover,

you will only have
to tackle one

or two last-minute chores

before you are ready to greet your guests.

Once everyone has arrived . . .

. . . it's time for
the feast.

For those not eager to
sink their teeth into
something new,

pizza will do.

Afterward, your friends will be dying
to see your room.

This is a terrific time
for makeovers.

Your guests will
love revamping
their looks for
the night.

But beware—
even if your guests
rave about dinner
and the fashion show
knocks them dead,

someone might start to feel homesick.

Remember—

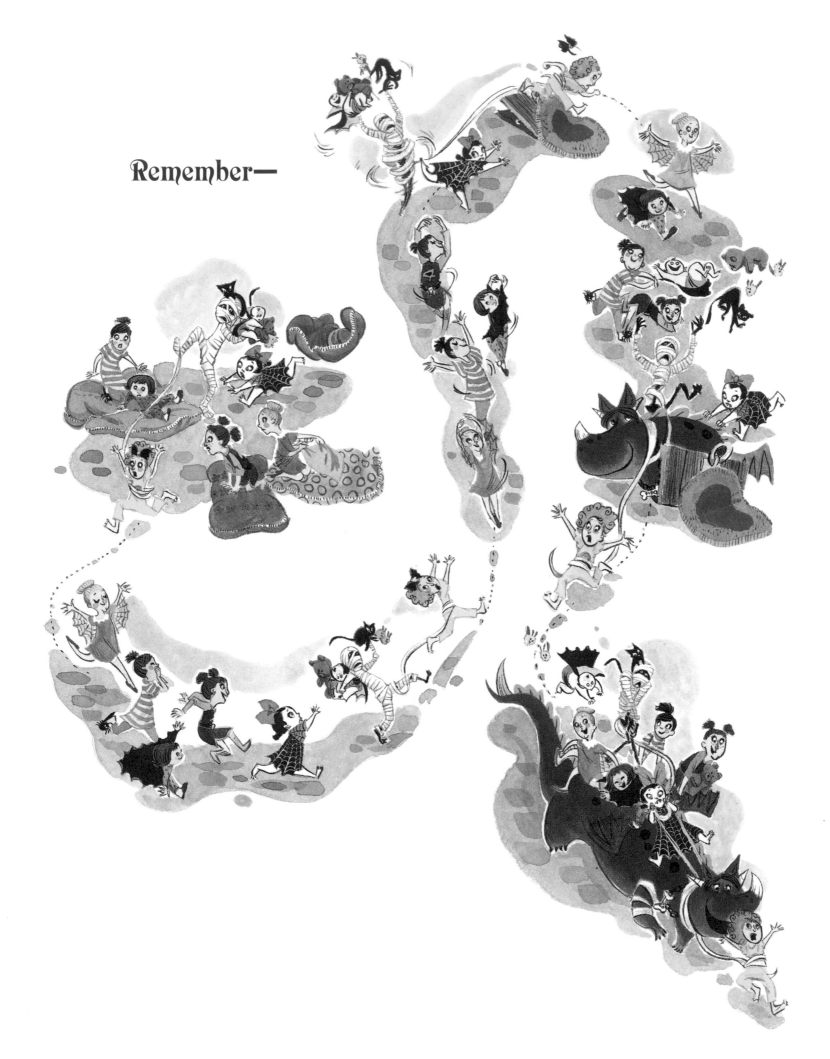

a true friend doesn't disappear
when a friend has trouble
with a new routine.

A true friend
remains on pointe

until the entire
ensemble

To keep your company in step, a scavenger hunt is the perfect pastime.

before you have
a chance

to dance,

is back on its feet.

Even though everyone is
having a blast,

dance,

DANCE!

Just don't let
anyone get carried
away . . .

your guests will eventually
grow weary.
Those who aren't sleepy
should find something quiet to do.

In the morning, it will be time for
your guests to depart.

Be sure to thank everyone for coming.

Then rest in peace,
satisfied that you have hosted
the Best Sleepover Ever!

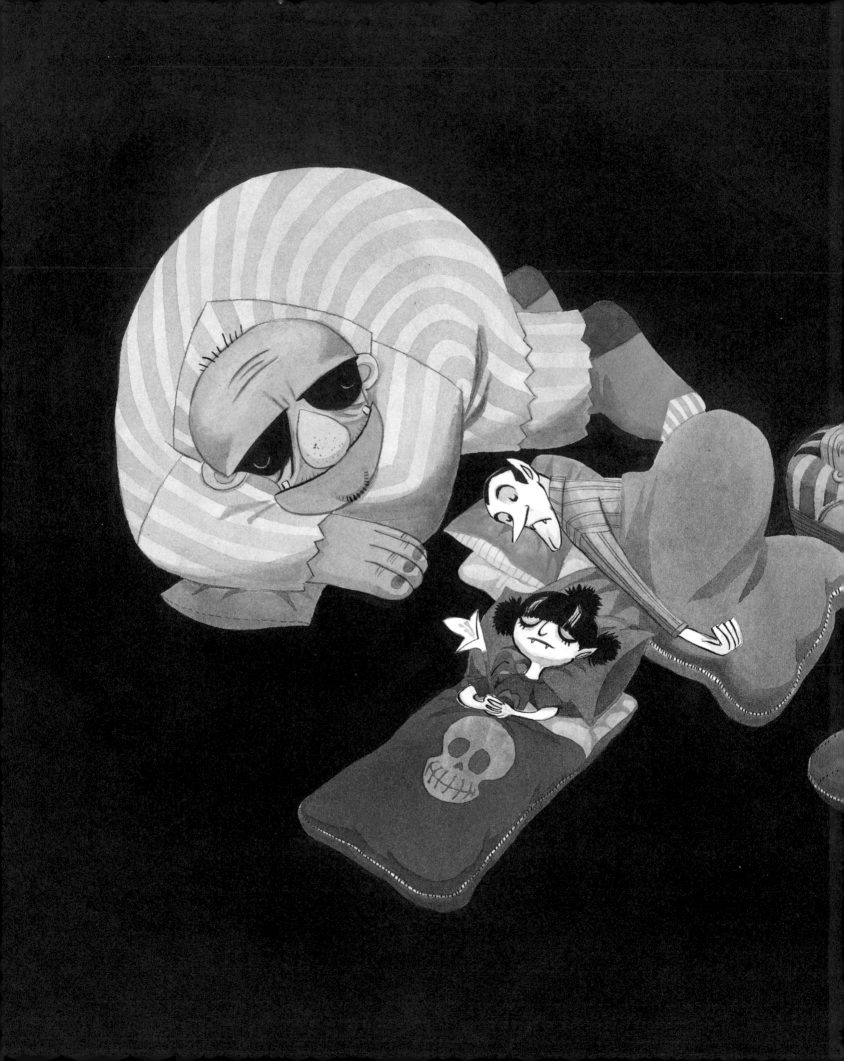